DINOSAURS
AFTER DARK

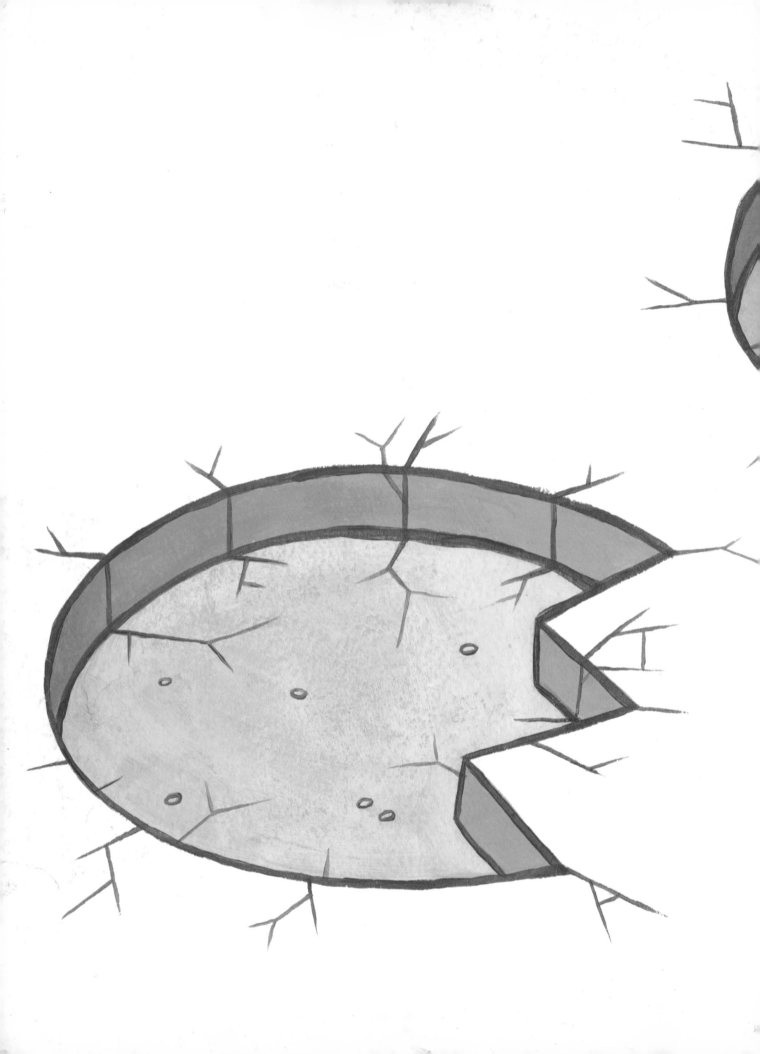

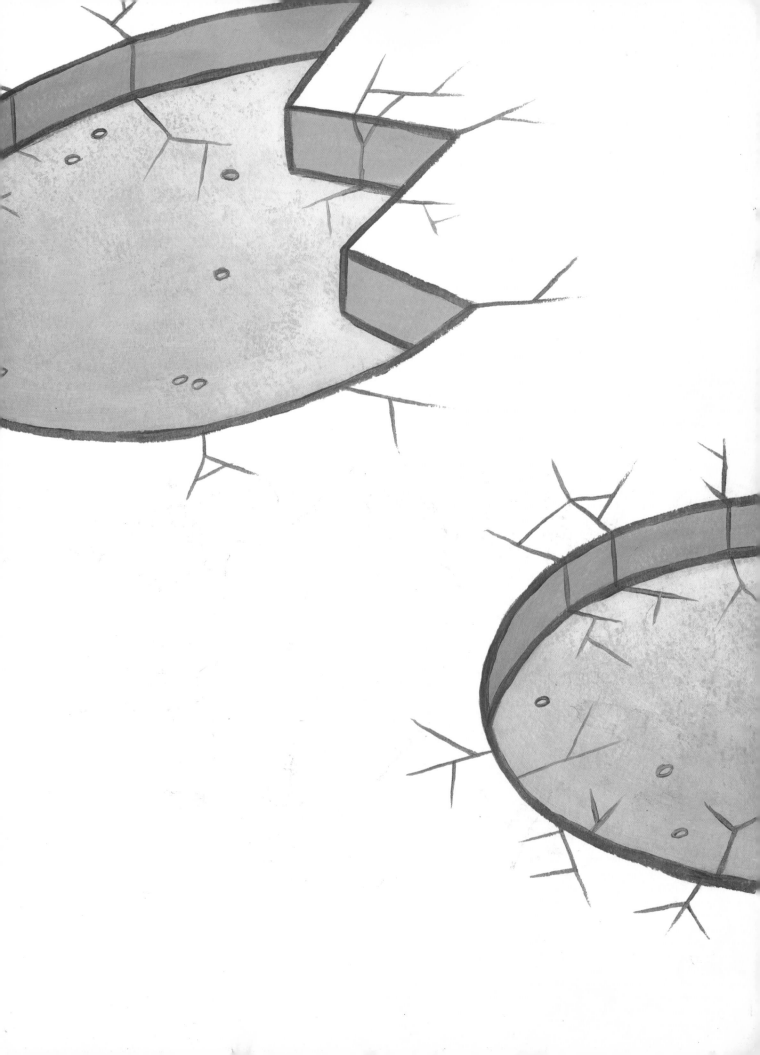

For Max, my consultant palaeontologist. J.E.
For Andrew, my beautiful boy. C.J.

First published in hardback in Great Britain by HarperCollins Publishers in 2001
First published in paperback by Collins Picture Books in 2003

1 3 5 7 9 10 8 6 4 2
ISBN: 000 664728 6

You can find out more about Jonathan Emmett's books
by visiting his website at www.scribblestreet.co.uk

DINOSAURS
AFTER DARK

Jonathan Emmett
and Curtis Jobling

Collins

An imprint of HarperCollinsPublishers

This is the story of Bobby who was lonely in the night.

And how when everyone else was sleeping, he heard the sound of something sneaking softly past his window.

And how he crept across the floor

and took a peep outside and saw . . .

a huge enormous

So Bobby grabbed his dressing gown,

and left his room   and tip-toed down the stairs

and through the hall,   out of the house into the city.

The monster crept from street to street,
and Bobby followed after it,

past unlit shops and office blocks,
and dark deserted buildings.

Until they reached the city square,

and DINOSAURS WERE EVERYWHERE!

But when they saw Bobby they roared
and ran after him chanting:

'Snatch him!'

'Munch him!'   'Catch him!'

'Crunch him!'

'Before he runs
and tells on us!'

But Bobby promised not to tell
and crossed it on his heart as well.

And so, instead of eating him, they let him join the fun.

Sliding down the rooftops above the City Hall,

climbing up the office blocks, then jumping off them all.

Splashing in the fountains and swinging from the cranes,

racing through the station and playing with the trains.

Underground and in the air,
those dinosaurs played everywhere!

'Now for one last game,' they cried,
'of hide and seek, and you can hide.'

'Yes, you can hide,
and we will seek you,

but if we find you,

we might

eat

you!'

So Bobby ran and ran and ran, until he found somewhere, snug and safe and secret, where nobody would find him!

And he curled up small and held his breath and listened for the sound of the dinosaurs' feet.

But all he heard was his own heart thumping, slower
and slower and slower . . .

until he fell fast asleep.

Then, someone did find him, and picked him up,
and carried him through the night, back to his bed,
where he sighed and smiled and slept . . .

...until morning.

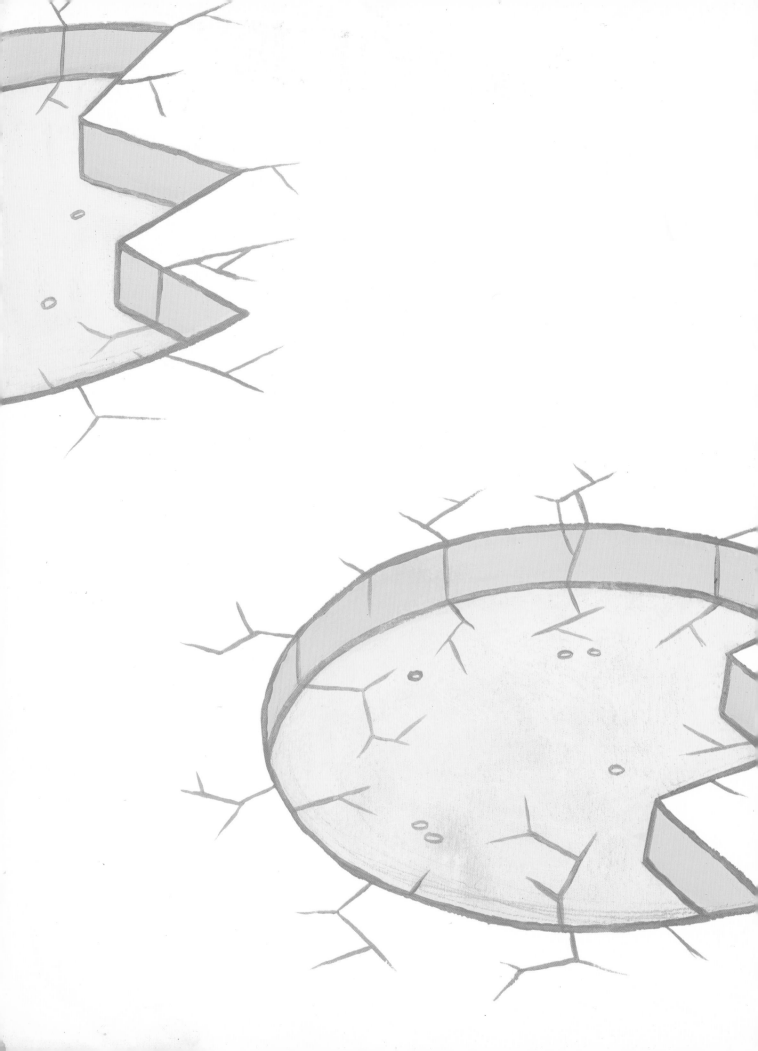

Every child deserves the best...

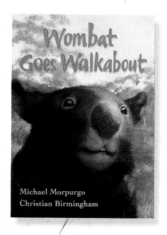

0-00-664627-1

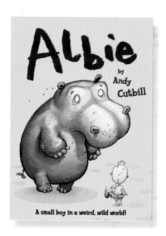

0-00-715002-4

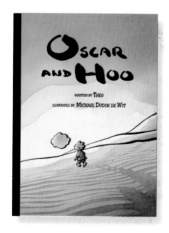

0-00-710794-3

0-00-713728-1

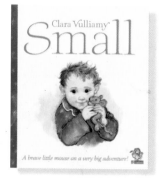

0-00-664775-8

0-00-710624-6

0-00-664777-4

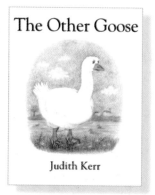

0-00-712735-9

0-00-714011-8

0-00-664646-8

Collins Picture Books